Dinosaur Alphabet

Written and illustrated by Harry S. Robins

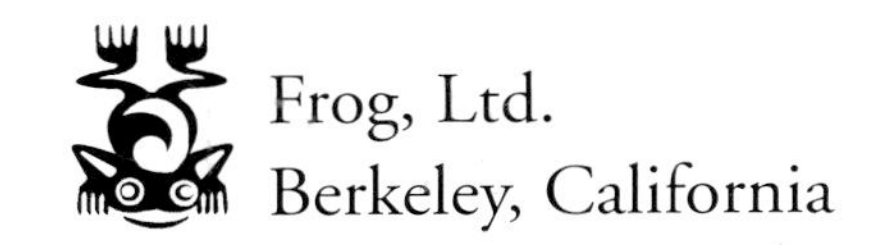

Frog, Ltd.
Berkeley, California

...paleontology requires that we consider not only discoveries, practices, and theories, but also imaginary constructs, because the role of fiction is constant both in the development of this science and its relationship to the public. The play of the imagination accompanies the discoveries, interpretations, and reconstructions of extinct beings.

—CLAUDINE COHEN, *The Fate of the Mammoth: Fossils, Myth, and History*

HOUGH IT DEPICTS AS WELL AS IT CAN, in picture and rhyme, the Mesozoic world of so many millions of years ago—a world over and done with, preserved in unchanging fossil mineral fragments—our understanding of the inhabitants of that ancient Earth continues to evolve. That is why very soon—probably already, in fact—the strictly scientific aspect of this book will become outdated, the fate of all dinosaur books. We are today in a period of rapid, accelerated learning about this period in our planet's remote past. Indeed, more new discoveries have been made during the last few decades than in the entire previous history of paleontology (and inevitably, we will find, so have more than a few new misconceptions and errors).

The dinosaurs, those intriguing extinct creatures, are therefore, paradoxically, now more alive than ever—in the human imagination. And as fresh knowledge comes, with it comes the license to dream, to make conjecture. What did they *really* look like? We will come closer and closer to the answers, yet we will never completely know for sure. But it is typical of our high-powered human curiosity to continue to try to visualize them as they might have been, just the same.

I know in my own case that it's a form of entertainment I have enjoyed for as long as I can remember: drawing dinosaurs, trying to make my pictures of them reflect what I understand to be the latest findings. In *Dinosaur Alphabet,* I have amused myself by recreating, *restoring,* as the term is, a different animal for each of the twenty-six letters. And perhaps this collection of decorated capitals, the Alphabet itself, will find other uses.

I'm assuming that most people who are drawn to this book probably already know something about dinosaurs. For the most part, the familiar names are not to be found here. Look in other books for the well-celebrated *Tyrannosaurus rex* and *Triceratops.* What you will find are some of their very close relations, though not all dinosaur types are represented. Here I am simply paying my respects to some personal favorites, a grouping that can only hint at the dazzling variety and prodigality, the inexhaustible creative ability of life on this earth.

Although no book can remain wholly accurate over time as more new discoveries are made, I have made an effort not to pass along misinformation in these pictures. The Notes following the main text offer various explanations, for those who are interested, of the choices I have made in depicting my subjects. Still, in preparing this book I have often been made uncomfortably aware of my own profound ignorance.

I do hope that *Dinosaur Alphabet* will aid whoever finds it to make an imaginary journey, to speculate and visualize the Earth's past, perhaps casting light on its possible future and the mystery of its purposes and development.

—H.R.

LLOSAURUS, forty feet
From toothy jaws to lashing tail,
Hunted game or carrion meat
Everywhere along the trail.

ARYONYX waited for a fish,
A soft-shelled turtle or a crab.
The waters served up every dish
His great-clawed hand or teeth could grab.

ERATOSAURUS, large of tooth
And long of tail, with serrate back
Was swift and fierce.
His horn, in truth
Suited display more than attack.

EINONYCHUS, with raptor squawks,
Pounces and slashes, tears and feeds,
Thinning the ranks of those she stalks—
Her great claw strikes down all she needs.

UOPLOCEPHALUS had grown
Along his length, from head to tail
An armored back of shields of bone,
A club to threaten or assail.

ABROSAURUS in her burrow,
Where she slept through months of drought,
Heard no more the hot sirocco;
Streams were running. She came out.

IGANOTOSAURUS, giant
Among predators, had teeth
Like sharpened arrowheads, compliant
Conquered flesh would yield beneath.

UAYANGOSAURUS sported
Plates up and spikes down his back;
Shoulder spears, it is reported
Made him harder to attack.

GUANODON snips with his beak
Of hardened horn the tender shoots.
Within the group the females seek
To herd their chicks with answering hoots.

OBARIA could rise upon
Massive hind legs to reach the top
Of towering trees, and batten on
The sweetest leaves to fill his crop.

ENTROSAURUS, crenellated
Mesozoic porcupine,
Predators shunned who evaded
Painful piercing from a spine.

LAMBEOSAURUS, on display,
Raised high in pride his head's dual crest.
Many a female looked his way...
Then, soon was spread another nest.

ONOCLONIUS cropped plants
With lowered beak, and waved his head.
His glittering eyes would often glance
Where the young females milled and fed.

With sturdy legs did
ODOSAURUS
Bear his heavy, armored bulk,
Plodding safely through the forest,
Well-defended walking hulk.

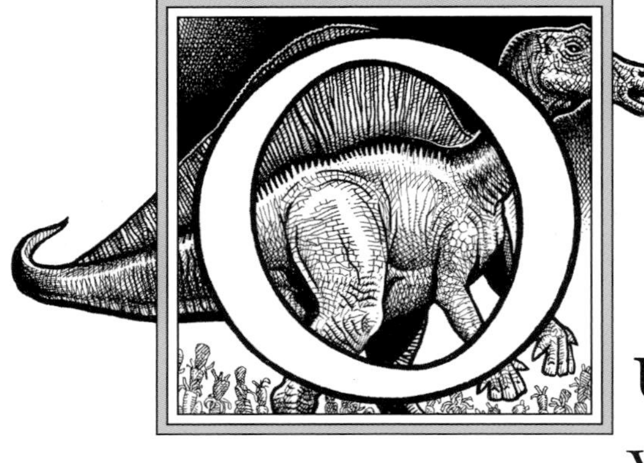

URANOSAURUS flushed his sail
With rose-red, beckoning the eyes
Of each female who raised her tail
And answered with resounding cries.

PLATEOSAURUS stretched her neck
Up to the fronds of tender green.
Long would be her descendants' trek,
The hugest walkers ever seen.

QUAESITOSAURUS hears quite well,
And as she browses, all the while,
She listens for the sounds that tell
Of theropod or crocodile.

HOETOSAURUS often wielded
Muscular and massive tail,
From the big meat-eaters shielded
By this bony club and flail.

Though
EISMOSAURUS shook the earth,
With gentle steps, from day to day,
She sought the uplands of her birth,
Devouring forests on her way.

OROSAURUS huge of head,
Shaking it, displays his horns;
With lengthy frill raised and outspread,
His ornate skull both shields and warns.

LTRASAUROS could face down
A giant carnivore alone;
Her massive bulk was carried on
Pillars of muscle, flesh, and bone.

ULCANODON was *très petite*
For sauropods, not quite a ton.
She cared not, basking in the heat
Of the still-young Jurassic sun.

UERHOSAURUS, stegosaur,
Bore dorsal plates like all his kin,
But each was smaller, low-slung, more
Like rectangle than tapering fin.

IAOSAURUS, fleet of foot,
Escaped the theropod's swift charge,
For far behind her she could put
Marauding creatures fierce and large.

ANGCHUANOSAURUS hid away
From the prey on which he dined,
Panting in the heat of midday,
Crouching in his hunter's blind.

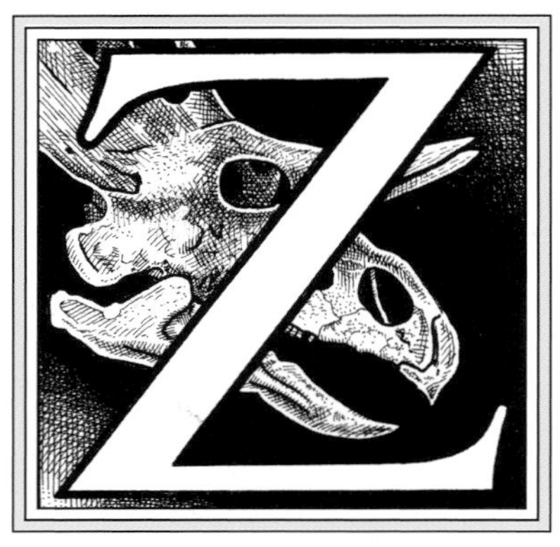
UNICERATOPS had lost
The group, her family, and her friends.
She heard, too late, and to her cost,
A heavy tread—the story ends.

Dimetrodon

Dimetrodon, an age before
There ever lived a dinosaur,
If dinosaur-like to human eyes
Stands closer to *us* in family ties,
Though in reptilian guise.

He was a *pelycosaur,* and we
Have found him near *our* family tree,
In Permian groves, where, dragon-like
He basked, before he'd hunt and strike.
His handsome shape we like.

Allosaurus *atrox*

Line 1 – *Forty feet.* The largest measurement recorded for the length of this animal is 39 feet (or about 12 meters), although the related *Epanterias* is thought to have been longer. I gave this one the extra foot, considering the extreme unlikelihood that every variation in size is represented in the fossil record.

Line 2 – *Lashing tail.* Allosaurs are classified within the family *tetanura,* "stiff-tails." It is thought that most of the long tail was not inclined to great flexion, though this is not completely certain. However, the tail could unquestionably bend at the base, and with great muscular force.

Though representation of this theropod in the largely discredited "kangaroo" posture of older paleontological restorations is discouraged, recent ichnological (footprint and trackway) evidence shows that some "carnosaurs" did assume it for at least part of the time, according to recently discovered tail drag marks.

Line 3 – *Hunted game or carrion meat.* A famous paleontologist stubbornly declares that all large theropods were "mere" scavengers, carrion-eaters, suggesting that their great size hobbled their potential as predators. Of course, this begs the question about how fast the prey itself might be moving. But I hold with the view that even the largest carnosaurs were agile hunters. Their mobility was perforce developed by evolution and their own practice, as they grew older and larger, to a very high degree, since at their adult size they could scarcely afford a single fall.

Then too, the distance between the hock, or heel, and the ground, one measure of potential speed for animals that walk on their toes, is significantly large in allosaurs. So they probably were fast enough to be the slayers their skeletons—in equipment and attitude—strongly suggest.

This being said, most animals do avoid working too hard whenever they can get away with it, and I can't see allosaurs being so over-fastidious as not to take up the gift of a nice, ripe carcass when they happened to encounter one.

Also pictured: a small reptile (a lepidosauriform sphenodontid), Jurassic insects, including a dragonfly and lepidopteran, and the pterosaur *Rhamphorhynchus.*

Baryonyx *walkeri*

From the Baremian of the early Cretaceous, excavated from the Wealden Formation of England, which is mentioned in A. Conan Doyle's *The Lost World.*

A spinosaur (possibly descended from dilophosaurs), *Baryonyx* was almost certainly a fish-eater. Crocodile-like jaws with a battery of an unusually large number of teeth and a deeply notched dilophosaur-like loose articulation near the tip of the snout both argue the case, and partly-digested fish scales were found inside the rib cage of the type specimen. But this was a massive land animal that probably devoured a wide variety of game as well. The neck of *Baryonyx* is without the strong S-curve usually found in theropods. Also pictured: *Lepidotes.*

CERATOSAURUS *nasicornis*

LINE 1 – *Large of tooth.* The teeth were disproportionately large, though the skull was lightly built.

LINE 2 – *Long of tail, with serrate back.* The tail in *Ceratosaurus* is indeed long, broad, and deep—and more than usually powerful. Vertebral spines along the thorax, pelvis, and tail are quite tall, almost finbacked. These tall spines were emphasized by a singular dorsal row of upstanding armor scutes of varying size, thought to be a primitive characteristic and also found on some sauropods *(Diplodocus).*

LINES 3, 4 – *His horn... suited display...* The extremely narrow horn might conceivably have aided in head-butting during mating controversies, but aside from that was likely mostly for show and no great tool of predation.

The arms and small four-fingered hands seem to have been of little use, but one can never tell. The avian-like wattle is a feature borrowed from an intriguing restoration by Josef Moravec. Also pictured: *Stegosaurus (stenops),* the small lacertan *Ardeosaurus* (a form of gecko), and the Jurassic lepidopteran *Kalligramma.*

DEINONYCHUS *antirrhopus*

LINE 3 – *Thinning the ranks of those she stalks...* A flock of dromeosaurs would indeed be a formidable agent of predation, culling the populations of other types in the field. Taxonomically the species is more properly considered to be within genus *Velociraptor.* Fearsomely armed, its structure a morphology at the extreme avian end of the phylogenetic bracket between birds and crocodiles, this creature is viewed by many as some sort of bird in fact. But it is simultaneously an 11-foot-long (3.35 meters) predatory dinosaur.

A large part of this length is the mostly rigid tail—the body had about the same mass as a big timber wolf of our own era. *Utahraptor,* a larger form, may possibly have had a nodular, tubercle-bearing or scale-like integument (although fossilized dinosaur skin indicates that scales *per se* were virtually unknown in Mesozoic dinosaurs), rather than the feathers shown here. The fossil evidence suggests to some that these carnivores hunted in packs and shared their food. The prey shown is the ornithischian dinosaur *Tenontosaurus tilleti.*

EUOPLOCEPHALUS *tutus*

LINE 3 – *An armored back of shields of bone.* The upper part of the beast's body—from the nose to the tail—was covered with bony plates studded with rows of horny spikes 4 to 6 inches (10 to 15 centimeters) long.

LINE 4 – *A club to threaten or assail.* Ankylosaurs like this one had a massive bony club at the end of the tail. The similar nodosaurs, who were otherwise very much like them, did not possess this weapon; the tail ended in the usual way (see *Nodosaurus,* below).

The club was a threat because it could assail in the creature's own defense. It was the business end of this well-fortified dinosaur. And the club made it too dangerous to attack. It could be lifted and swung as depicted, but it was also a menace carried at a lower level where it could deal telling blows against the legs and ankles of carnosaurs—something to be avoided at all costs, since serious injury to these essential parts was a virtual death sentence.

For extra insurance, *Euoplocephalus* was armed as well as dangerous. Once thought to be the same as *Ankylosaurus,* the animal is very similar to that most famous of Ankylosaurs in having dorsal armor plate on body and four-"horned" head. Even the eyelids were armored. The name *Euoplocephalus,* in fact, means "well-armed head" (Greek *euloplo-* = well-armed + *kephale* = head).

Two possible views of the dermal armor and club are shown here. In the main illustration, the ankylosaur is rebuffing the tyrannosaur *Alioramus,* who should have known better.

Fossils of *Euoplocephalus* have been found in Alberta, Canada. *Enodontosaurus, Dyoplosaurus,* and *Scolosaurus* are other names given to fossil remains that are now considered to be the same as *Euoplocephalus.*

FABROSAURUS *australis (Lesothosaurus)*

LINES 1–2 – *in her burrow / Where she slept…* Did this small Triassic dinosaur have dormant periods, or aestivate? (To say *hibernate* would give the false suggestion of a "winter" season.) The speculation has been made. Drawing this conclusion from dental growth patterns, paleontologist Tony Thulborn posited *Fabrosaurus* as able to withstand periods of draught by hibernating.

Many contemporary animals do this, from bears to toads. Secluding one's self in a burrow would also be an additional strategy for avoiding large predators, besides the far more common one of simply outrunning them.

An aspect of the skull suggests that there may have been a salt gland; like seagulls, elephants, crocodiles, and humans, this small dinosaur may have eliminated excess salt by shedding tears.

Unlike other ornithischians, the fabrosaurids did not have cheek pouches.

Fabrosaurids may have given rise to all of the later ornithischan dinosaurs. See *Xiaosaurus,* below.

The extant fossil material is minimal and fragmentary, and *Fabrosaurus* has become a somewhat general name for this type of ornithischian, in the same way that some of us now like to call diplodocid sauropods "brontosaurs," even though the old genus name *Brontosaurus* has been (sadly) retired. *Fabrosaurus,* in truth, may not be significantly different from *Lesothosaurus.* Perhaps this is that creature.

Giganotosaurus *carolinii*

Line 1 – *giant.* Discovered in 1994 in Patagonia, a region of Argentina, this huge carnivore, at an estimated 50-plus feet (15-plus meters) in overall length, was larger than any of the known specimens of *Tyrannosaurus rex,* the previous record-holder for almost 90 years as the biggest terrestrial meat-eater ever. The king is dead, long live the king!

The famous *Tyrannosaurus* is now classified as an enlarged form of dromeosaur (see *Deinonychus,* above), but the truly gigantic *Giganotosaurus* is apparently an enormous allosaur, like another recently (re-)discovered carnosaur, the African *Carcharodontosaurus,* also bigger and bulkier than T-rex.

Also pictured: a justifiably terrified *Hypsilophodon.*

Huayangosaurus *taibaii*

Lines 3–4 – *Shoulder spears… made him harder to attack.* I take the view (see *Kentrosaurus,* below) that at least some of this impressive weaponry was practical, and not *only* for the all-important function of sexual display, e.g. looking good to appraising females.

The "spears" were probably located on the shoulders. If not, they then most likely protruded from the hips. When presented with a jumble of disarticulated bones, one can only guess. The flattened base of these elongated spikes must have rested either against the outer surface of the pelvis or upon the scapula, or shoulder blade. Perhaps some stegosaurs had hip spikes *(Kentrosaurus, Paranthodon)* while others *(Lexovisaurus)* sported shoulder spikes? A recently unearthed Asian stegosaur, *Chialingosaurus,* seems to have had wing-like plates, not spikes, projecting from the shoulders above the forelegs. Another, *Gigantospinosaurus sichuanensis,* had record-holding shoulder spine "wings" facing upward and back, the largest known on any stegosaur to date, making it look like a monster from a Japanese movie!

Stegosaurs are found in two subgroups, or families. The smaller of the two is the Huayangosauridae, of which *Huayangosaurus* is the chief representative.

One thing *Huayangosaurus* had that is unusual for stegosaurs is small teeth in the front of the upper jaw, rather than the usual toothless beak.

A diminutive but belligerent *Sinosauropteryx,* another Asian dinosaur, momentarily confronts *Huayangosaurus.*

IGUANODON *mantellii*

LINE 3 – *Within the group.* At one time it was said dismissively, "reptiles don't herd." Dinosaurs were thought to be dull-witted single wanderers, "roaming the earth." But (A) dinosaurs *aren't* "reptiles" like many of our familiar existing types, but more like, in my view, a special derived kind of super-reptiles; (B) anyway, some reptiles *do* herd, or at least form aggregate societies or colonies. And in fact, living crocodiles care for their young for a time.

However the mental capacities of dinosaurs may be reckoned, the work of John R. Horner and others has strongly suggested that some ornithischians (the now well-known *Maiasaura peeblesorum* in particular) practiced social behavior in the herd as well as extended parental care. And where roaming the earth is concerned, while foraging they probably did plenty of that.

Since 1878, *Iguanodon* has often been found preserved in large groups, and is usually now represented as a social creature, a characterization fossil trackways also strongly suggest. It was the second dinosaur to be named scientifically, after *Megalosaurus,* in 1824.

JOBARIA *tiguidensis*

LINE 1 – *could rise.* There seems to be no doubt that this sauropod could get up on its hind legs, giving it a feeding advantage despite its relatively short neck, which was composed of only twelve vertebrae. The African *Jobaria's* backbone and tail are simple compared to the complex vertebrae and whiplash tail of the older, North-American sauropods *Diplodocus* and *Apatosaurus.* Unlike other Cretaceous sauropods, *Jobaria* has spoon-shaped teeth.

Jobaria, discovered in 1997, does not fit into any recognized family of long-necked dinosaurs. Rather, it represents an ancient lineage that survived and flourished only in Africa during the Cretaceous Period.

It's a curious thing. We know the image of *Brontosaurus,* which many of us grew up with in the fifties and earlier as *the* typical sauropod, has been dismissed. The creature everybody thought of as *Brontosaurus,* the "thunder lizard," actually, they say, held its neck lower, and had a different skull and a longer, more gracile tail. (And of course the name *Brontosaurus* no longer applies and has been retired in favor of the less euphonious *Apatosaurus.)* But here is a fine big dinosaur—adults were around 60 feet (18.3 meters) long, quite big enough to thunder—astonishingly like the old-style Bronto in most particulars: the *Camarasaurus*-like head carried high on a shorter neck, the rounded, arched back, the robust tail apparently carried with a downward turn (though naturally it didn't drag). So if you, like me, from time to time miss old *Brontosaurus,* be consoled—we do have *Jobaria.*

KENTROSAURUS *aethiopicus*

LINE 2 – *Mesozoic porcupine.* Not that *Kentrosaurus* "threw" its "quills" or acted particularly porcupine-like, but my guess is that this smallish, 14-and-a-half-foot (about 4.5 meters) stegosaur's spikes, which extended from the tail to the high point over the hips, actually did have value as defensive structures beyond their utility in species recognition and sexual display. This would also be true of the flank spikes, whether they belong properly at the shoulders or the hips, where I have shown them. (See *Huayangosaurus)*

Plates and spikes, or spines, are apparently paired in this case, not alternated as are the plates in *Stegosaurus.* This arrangement of the dermal armor in some stegosaurs is still being debated.

In the distance, a ceratosaur eyes a potentially unpalatable meal speculatively.

Also known as *Kentrurosaurus.*

LAMBEOSAURUS *lambei*

LINE 1 – *on display.* The curious crest on this hadrosaur (from the Oldman Formation in western Alberta, Canada) helped identify it for others of its species. This, as I've noted elsewhere, was probably the primary function of all dinosaurian ornamentation. Most of the Oldman duck-billed dinosaurs had distinctive head crests; some examples are the closely related *Lambeosaurus magnicristatus* and *Corythosaurus.*

But the crest did have at least one other function as part of the distinctive architecture of the skull, harboring elongated passages within the nasal and premaxillary bones. These were resonating chambers that enabled the dinosaur to make a special identifying sound when a hadrosaur wished to defend its territory.

The tail of *Lambeosaurus* was stiffened all along its length by a system of crisscrossing support rods, a sort of evolutionary retrofit. Only the tip of the tail, some think, had any chance of flexibility.

Monoclonius *nasicornis*

Lines 2–4 – *...his head... the young females.* The squamosoparietal frill, or "shield," and the long nasal horn, which could point forward or upward and back in different specimens, probably had some use in intra-species aggression, though it's less easy to suggest a similar function for the smaller horns at the back of the shield. Principally, these features together served to identify and distinguish the most-ornamented male as a breeding advantage, as was the case with most dinosaur ornamentation.

Much scientific opinion is that *Monoclonius* is a misnomer for the similar *Centrosaurus,* and should be looked upon as a dubiously named dinosaur. However, this is not the opinion of Professor Peter Dodson, one of paleontology's foremost authorities on the Ceratopsians. He differentiates this species from *Centrosaurus* in his book *The Horned Dinosaurs,* even suggesting that *Centrosaurus* will in time prove to be the invalid name. So I feel better about including *Monoclonius* here.

Nodosaurus *textilis*

Line 4 – *Well-defended.* This dinosaur seems to have been largely without weapons of aggression (although this isn't fully known since its remains are fragmentary and scarce). To survive in a world of large, fierce predators it had to have, then, a good defense. This was in the form of transverse bands of heavy body armor from head to tail, each flat-lying plate studded with a knob, or *node,* the basis of the animal's name.

Nodosaurus was an ankylosaur, a member of the larger group the Thyreophora or "shield-bearers." There were two main subgroups of ankylosaurs, the Nodosaurids

(*Nodosaurus* is eponymous) and the Ankylosaurids. The diagnostic difference between the two is that ankylosaurs had a distinctive weapon, a bony "club," or mace, at the end of the tail (see *Euoplocephalus,* above), while nodosaurs did not.

I am of the opinion that almost all dinosaurs used their tails as weapons, including *Nodosaurus.* Probably the tail club of the later ankylosaurs developed as a refinement, and a successful one, since with its aid they lasted the whole way to the end of the Age of Reptiles, when the curtain descended on the dinosaurs at the close of the Cretaceous.

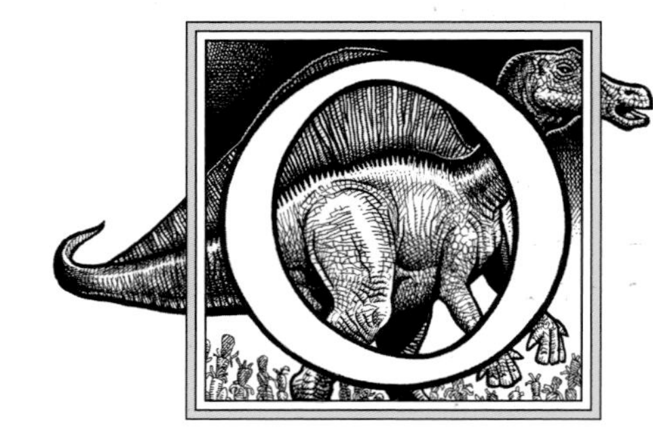

OURANOSAURUS *nigeriensis*

LINE 1 – *flushed his sail.* Among the ornithopods, the iguanodontids (see *Iguanodon,* above) had horse-like, elongated snouts ending in broad, toothless horny beaks. They had distinctive five-fingered hands. The three middle digits ended in hoof-like processes; the first, or thumb, was a pointed spike not used for locomotion—perhaps it was a food-gathering aid or even, some think, a weapon. The outer finger had greater flexibility.

Ouranosaurus had these features, and though noticeably more gracile than *Iguanodon,* clearly belongs with the iguanodontids—the skeleton is very similar. What really sets it apart, though, is the spectacular "sail" on its back, actually closer to a hump than to a fin. If you look at the skeleton of an American bison or a camel you will see a similar structure. The hump, or sail, of *Ouranosaurus* was made from skin and fat stretched over the greatly elongated dorsal spinal processes. This skin is thought to have been richly supplied with blood vessels.

One theory cites the whole structure as a heat-exchanging device to regulate body temperature—depending on its angle to the sun, blood drawn into the sail would either radiate or capture heat. That could be true, I suppose, although *Ouranosaurus* lived in the blazing Mesozoic tropics and I think having to *avoid* the sun all the time would have been a nuisance for this largish (23 feet or 7 meters in length) dinosaur.

My guess is that the creature "displayed" with his sail, making it change color to attract the attention of prospective mates.

Line 4 – *who raised their tails.* Many ornithischian dinosaurs (see *Lambeosaurus,* above) seem to have been limited in their abilities to move their tails laterally.

In ornithischians, transverse stiffening rods locked the vertebrae into place. But though *Ouranosaurus* had these rods, they mostly supported the sail, although they did extend posteriorly just past the base of the tail. This suggests the rest of the tail could have been bendable from side to side.

But what about up-and-down movement? I was once able to ask Dr. John "Jack" Horner, a renowned authority on ornithopods, whether he thought they could lift and lower their tails. His emphatic answer was that they could not. (And though saurischian dinosaurs could, he stated, they "wouldn't want to.")

I'm not disputing Dr. Horner, a true expert. When I say ouranosaurs raised their tails, I only mean that they elevated them by bending their arms when on all fours. That's all it would take.

In a sheltered canyon out of the heat, three ouranosaurs socialize. In the left foreground is a long-tailed Cretaceous freshwater turtle, *Clemmys.* In the air are a single pterosaur, *Ornithodesmus latidens* (not a full-grown specimen) and various enantiornithine birds, including *Iberomesornis* and *Eoalulavis.* Modern bird groups developed in the Eocene; these Mesozoic types, with three grasping fingers on the leading edge of the wing, were found on an evolutionary side branch, as it were. *Iberomesornis* had teeth in its bill and, it is thought, did not retract its legs when in flight in the manner of modern birds.

PLATEOSAURUS *longiceps*

LINES 3–4 – *their descendants... the hugest walkers... Plateosaurus* was already respectably big for its time (the early to middle Triassic) and was the first really large dinosaur—more than 26 feet (8 meters) in length, it weighed in at around 1,500 pounds (three quarters of a ton or more than 680 kilograms). It was a prosauropod, (roughly) ancestral to the giant sauropods, as the group name suggests. *Plateosaurus,* they say, could assume a bipedal stance to feed on high-growing plants. (Some who have thought the creature's diet included meat, however, have cited the serrated teeth of *Plateosaurus* as evidence for this claim.)

The exact evolutionary place of this dinosaur is not clear, but it appeared along with the other prosauropods, some of which were in truth very sauropod-like. The body type does seem to suggest the giants of a later age, who for the size of land animals have never been surpassed.

Plateosaurus had three major and two minor toes on each hind foot. The manus, or hand, also had five digits, which bore curving claws.

A dragonfly, *Protolibellula,* is at left, and the late Triassic rhamphorhynchoid pterosaur *Peteinosaurus zambelli* soars on the right.

QUAESITOSAURUS *orientalis*

LINE 1 – *hears quite well...* The skull indicates that this dinosaur did have good hearing, since a large tympanic opening and robust auditory chamber would have helped sounds resonate within.

Fossil remains of enormous sauropod dinosaurs are often found without the head, which is small and insignificant when compared to the outsized bulk of the body. But *Quaesitosaurus* is known *only* from the head. Long, low, and horse-like with frontally located peg-like teeth, it is similar enough to the skulls of *Diplodocus* and its kin to have prompted informed speculation that the missing body was formed like those of diplodocids. Extrapolation from the proportions of the fossil material suggests that the overall length of the creature may have been about 43 feet, or 13 meters.

Line 4 – *theropod or crocodile.* The long-necked sauropods flourished in the Jurassic period, but some types, including *Quaesitosaurus,* were successful enough to make it all the way on into the late Cretaceous.

In the middle Campanian and early Maastrichtian ages even these fair-sized sauropods would have had to contend with large predators such as the *Albertosaurus*-like tyrannosaurid theropod shown at left or the gigantic crocodilian *Deinosuchus,* until recently called *Phobosuchus,* seen sneaking up on the right.

Monster crocs like *Deinosuchus,* at an estimated 43 feet (13 meters) long, or the even larger African *Sarcosuchus* were ambush predators like the modern Nile Crocodile or its fellow giant the Mugger of India. Lying hidden in the water before lunging out to take prey, these beasts are thought to have included in their diet, besides fish of a certain size and various swimming reptiles, big dinosaurs—when they could get them.

It is possible that *Nemegtosaurus,* also known only from skull material, is a very close relative of *Quaesitosaurus,* if not indeed a variation of the same animal.

Rhoetosaurus *brownei*

Line 4 – *this bony club and flail. Rhoetosaurus* comes to us in the Hutton Sandstone Formation of Queensland, Australia, from the Bajocian Age of the Dogger Epoch, 181–175 million years ago. Its robust tailbones indicate that the whole tail, which swiftly tapered, was considerably well-muscled. To some this has suggested that at the tip there may have been a bony club to swing against attackers.

Such an inference is not as outlandish as it might once have seemed. The similar sauropod *Shunosaurus* is known to have had such a club. This was a most surprising discovery at the time. Traditionally sauropods, saurischians, were not supposed to have features found on ornithischians, among them tail clubs and body armor. But it seems some of them did; *Saltasaurus* and the Cretaceous titanosaurid *Chubutisaurus* had bony plates set in the skin, for example. So the ornithischian and saurischian groups did have some crossover features.

Well, in all fairness, I must admit that no tail club has actually been found among the fragmentary remains of *Rhoetosaurus.* But others have theorized that it may have been present, and I like the idea.

SEISMOSAURUS *hallorum*

LINES 1–2 – *shook the earth... with gentle steps... Seismo* is the Latin root for "shaking," encountered in *seismic, seismologist,* and all words relating to earth movement.

Since *Seismosaurus* probably weighed 100 tons or more, like other super-giant sauropods, it's not unlikely that if one walked in your vicinity you would know about it.

And yet, it could be that this colossal creature strolled relatively softly, with its padded heels and its walk cycle of moving one immense leg at a time. Percussive stamping would involve powerful forces that might prove inimical to the well-being of such a big animal.

Still, the dramatic concept of the earth-shaking dinosaur, also and most famously expressed in the no longer official name *Brontosaurus,* is still too aesthetically attractive to relinquish.

LINES 3–4 – *She sought the uplands... devouring forests...* Whether or not *Seismosaurus* traveled in groups, as many think, continuous wandering was a necessity for this kind of creature; even the fecund and abundant Mesozoic world couldn't locally supply the dietary needs and appetite of a solitary one of these giants. Constantly walking, eating, and digesting, a single *Seismosaurus,* let alone a "herd," would have had a devastating effect on whatever stands of vegetation it happened to encounter. In this context a migratory pattern of some sort makes sense, and breeding and egg-laying would have their place within that pattern.

Seismosaurus was a diplodocid sauropod, perhaps just a giant form of the already giant *Diplodocus.* Its estimated length of 150 feet, or 45.72 meters, makes it the longest, though not the most massive dinosaur known to science. (That distinction would be held by one of the larger forms of *Brachiosaurus* or the recently discovered *Argentinosaurus.*)

The tail, 70 feet (21.34 meters) long, had a downward bend about 14 feet (4.27 meters) along its length from the hips, probably an adaptation to lower the center of gravity. I have shown the forepart of the neck flexible enough to allow the head to turn and look backward. If the anterior portion of the neck could bend, the middle part is thought to be fairly stiff. Elongated cervical processes, which braced the neck, may have significantly limited possible movement. Of course, such soft tissues as tendons, intervertebral discs, and synovial joints and ligaments may have allowed a range of motion that osteology alone might appear to forbid.

TOROSAURUS *latus*

LINE I – *huge of head.* The largest *Torosaurus* skull, at 8-and-a-half feet, or about 2.6 meters, was considered for many years the biggest of any land animal. Then, an even larger ceratopsian skull—that of a *Pentaceratops*—turned up to dispute the record-holder. But the most recent findings re-establish the preeminence of *Torosaurus* with the recovery of a skull nearly 9 feet (2.7 meters) long and, at its widest part, 8 feet (2.4 meters) wide. And so it goes.

Torosaurus, one of the last dinosaurs to live on Earth, may have been the largest of the horned ceratopsians or ceratopians, with a body larger than that of the famous *Triceratops.*

Most pictures of this creature, even in very recently published dinosaur books, are incorrect. They show the long squamosoparietal shield, or frill, as smooth-edged, without the epoccipital bones that distinguish *Triceratops* and other ceratopsians. This frill is traditionally restored as lying flat over the shoulders of the animal and slightly heart-shaped at the top. But that concept turns out to be based on incomplete fossil material, mostly collected during the nineteenth century, pieced together with guesswork and plaster.

It has been established that the skull was not as long as originally thought, not smooth-edged but rimmed with around twenty-four epoccipitals. We now believe the frill has a slight diamond shape at the top, and curls up behind the horns at roughly a 35-degree angle.

The canonical *Triceratops,* most familiar of the ceratopsian dinosaurs, is unusual in having a solid frill; most ceratopsids had fenestrae, or openings, in this impressive feature of the extended skull. *Torosaurus* was no exception. But these apertures in *Torosaurus* are smaller than often shown in various restorations, and rounder, almost circular.

Some generally assume that the name *Torosaurus* comes from *toro,* the Spanish word for bull, and signifies "bull lizard." Well, the beast may indeed have been a sort of Mesozoic bull, but actually, that name would have to be *Tauro-saurus.* The Greek root of the name lies in *torus,* referring to perforation—the two paired round holes, or parietal fenestrae (they were covered by hide in life), in the shield.

ULTRASAUROS *macintoshi*

LINE 1 – *could face down.* Being taller than everybody else has its uses, and one use is that in the animal world superior height intimidates.

Ultrasauros, a prodigy of size among brachiosaurs—which are already known for being monstrously huge—may have been able to bluff its most serious enemies and rivals by looking down on them. *Brachiosaurus* and its kin held their heads high.

But *Ultrasauros,* formerly *Ultrasaurus* (it was re-named in 1991 to avoid confusion with another, smaller brachiosaur also, it turned out, named *Ultrasaurus*) is known from fragmentary material and may not have been a brachiosaur at all, but more of a diplodocid. Although the scapula, or shoulder blade, seems to suggest a brachiosaur affinity, there is a theory that the known vertebrae and partial pelvis may have been from *Supersaurus,* a giant sauropod thought to belong among the relatives of *Diplodocus.*

Whether brachiosaur, diplodocid, or something in between, *Ultrasauros* was *big;* one estimate of its weight that has been made is an astonishing 130 tons. At that size it would have been intimidating all right, and, one may suppose, very likely able to raise its head high enough to look down on other dinosaurs.

Here *Ultrasauros* looks down on the carnivore *Eustreptospondylus* (27 feet or 8 meters long), as on the right, *Elaphrosaurus,* a coelurosaur-ceratosaur hybrid, and the small meat-eater *Ornitholestes* flee the scene.

VULCANODON *karibaensis*

LINES 1–2 – très petite *for sauropods. Vulcanodon* lived in the very early Jurassic, among prosauropods in fact, in the Hettangian Age in the lowest part of the Lias Epoch.

Indeed, the hipbones of *Vulcanodon* show some features similar to those of prosauropods like *Plateosaurus,* above. But unlike *Plateosaurus,* a sometime biped, *Vulcanodon* had pillar-like forelimbs which were totally graviportal, or weight-supporting, in function. For *Vulcanodon* was no prosauropod but an actual, elegant little sauropod, to our eyes scaled down from the giants of the later Jurassic and Cretaceous but just the same a pioneer in their early evolution.

WUERHOSAURUS *homheni*

LINE 1 – *stegosaur…* Like most others in the stegosaur group, this dinosaur had forelegs far smaller than the pillar-like hind legs, so that the hips were twice as high as the shoulders. Its wedge-shaped head began with a hard beak and its tail terminated in the usual stegosaurian spikes.

There are at least two things that distinguish *Wuerhosaurus* within the rank of stegosaurs. One is that it lived in the early Cretaceous, significantly after the stegosaurs' heyday; it's found in rocks around 140–130 million years old. Most stegosaurids thrived in the Jurassic, a much earlier time at around 160–144 million years ago. So *Wuerhosaurus,* a robust type nearly as large (26 feet or 8 meters) as the eponymous *Stegosaurus,* stands as one of the last of these great plated dinosaurs.

LINES 2–3 – *…bore dorsal plates…But each was smaller…* The other distinguishing feature of *Wuerhosaurus* is the lower and flatter-topped back plate array. These gave a distinctive silhouette for all-important infra-species recognition.

But the stubby, almost rectangular plates are ill-suited to prove other popular theories about stegosaur plate functions. As defensive armor they are not very impressive. And the speculation that stegosaur plates helped regulate body heat, either by radiating it in wind and shadow or gathering it from direct solar exposure, doesn't really seem viable with these small-surfaced ornaments of *Wuerhosaurus.*

Actually, stegosaur plates were not fully vascularized in any case. Blood did not totally circulate through them back into the body of the animal. Unfortunately for the traditional heat-exchange theory, blood flowed into but not out of the plates at their bases, supporting their rapid growth.

Xiaosaurus *dashanpensis*

Line 1 – *fleet of foot. Xiaosaurus* was a little plant-eater, just under 5 feet (about 1.5 meters) long (and about half of this was the tail), that lived in Asia during the mid-Jurassic period, 178 million years ago. These quick dinosaurs probably lived in large family groups and moved through thick forests to keep hidden. They had very little else that we know of in the way of defenses against a world of predators.

The relative proportions of the lower limb bones and the runner's foot of *Xiaosaurus* tell this story.

Xiaosaurus is tentatively placed between the early herbivore *Lesothosaurus* (see *Fabrosaurus,* above) and *Hypsilophodon,* a progenitor of *Iguanodon.* It also had some primitive attributes found on basal ornithischians. A transitional type, *Xiaosaurus* was an ornithopod (the bird-footed, beaked, bipedal, herbivorous dinosaurs), belonging to the family *Fabrosauridae.*

In the picture two *Xiaosaurus* flee from a dilophosaur, a crested carnivore. *Dilophosaurus sinensis* is known from the Lower Jurassic of China.

Yangchuanosaurus *shanguensis*

Line 4 – *his hunter's blind.* Although the mounted skeleton in the Beijing Museum of Natural History is in excess of 21 feet, or more than 6.5 meters, still larger forms have been found exceeding 33 feet (10.06 meters), making this allosaur relative a good-sized theropod. Just the same, it doesn't seem unreasonable to suppose that it may have been an ambush predator, despite its size finding concealment from which to rush out, at the crucial moment, to take down the young of large dinosaurs or moderately sized adults.

Conversely, it might have hunted in groups to attack even the biggest dinosaurs. Or, it may have been exclusively a carrion-feeder. Speculations like mine about its patterns of behavior are no more than that.

I collect plastic dinosaur figures, and have a *Yangchuanosaurus* among them. Such models are often defective in representing the feet properly, and I thought when I examined this one that the sculptor had carelessly left out the reduced first toe, found on allosaurs and their relatives. But contrary to many portrayals of the animal I have seen displayed on the Internet, which give it the standard allosaur foot, it turns out that *Yangchuanosaurus,* as on my accurate little model, did indeed have just three digits on each of its four limbs, every one armed with a claw.

The potential *Yangchuanosaurus* dinner shown is the stegosaur *Tuojiangosaurus multispinus,* which is quite similar to the canonical *Stegosaurus,* although the back plates are smaller, narrower, and more pointed.

ZUNICERATOPS *christopheri*

LINE 2 – *the group…Zuniceratops* was an early horned dinosaur, on a nearby side branch of the evolutionary tree that produced *Triceratops* and the great Ceratopsian horn-and-shield-bearers of the later Cretaceous. These more recent giant beasts have often been found with their bodies crowded together. Though not, strictly speaking, ancestral to this clade, little *Zuniceratops,* I am supposing, probably also was apt to find safety in numbers.

Gracile compared with the ornate behemoths of a later age (see *Monoclonius* and *Torosaurus*), *Zuniceratops* comes, by way of a few scattered bones, from the Turonian or lower upper Cretaceous, 91–85 million years before the present day.

LINE 4 – *A heavy tread…* Large carnivores from the Turonian are poorly known, but you may depend on it that they were always on the scene, including early tyrannosaurids. These progenitors of the famous *Tyrannosaurus rex* evolved from dromeosaur ancestors.

(Barely) known from the Turonian-Santonian is the predator *Itemirus medullaris,* which I have speculatively restored here as the agent of *Zuniceratops's* downfall.

Among the fragments comprising the type specimen of *Itemirus* is the braincase, which is quite similar in many particulars to that of the smaller *Stokesosaurus clevelandi,* an advanced tyrannosaurid. From this I infer that the ferocious *Itemirus* was well along the way to expressing the vigor and power of this group of carnivores.

Other evidence suggests a very dromeosaurid tyrannosaurid, and though I have given him an aspect like that of *Albertosaurus* and a hand in transition, with a dwindling third digit, to that of the two-fingered tyrannosaurs, I think I would restore him with a rigid tail and provide the foot, not visible in the picture, with a scaled-up version of the terrible slashing claw of the dromeosaurs, like the ones you can see clearly in the picture of *Deinonychus.*

# Acknowledgments

I am among many whose interest in all things dinosaurian and prehistoric was sparked at a very early and impressionable age by the fabulous imagery of pioneering paleo-artists, the great Charles R. Knight and Zdeněk Burian foremost among them. I would also be remiss not to mention the endless inspiration provided by the stop-motion films of Willis O'Brien, Phil Tippett, and Ray Harryhausen.

This book's creation and development were eased by the patient encouragement of some whom it would be wrong not to thank. To Emily Boyd, my project editor at Frog, Ltd., particularly gracious and helpful during the later stages of this little volume's gestation, I wish to note my appreciation here. Thanks are certainly due for the many useful suggestions and help during production given by Vicki Olds of Studio Reflex. Tracy Feldstein offered real assistance and support when it was most needed, and helped me through many difficulties.